Jerry Spinelli

Other titles in the *Authors Teens Love* series:

Ray Bradbury
Master of Science Fiction and Fantasy
ISBN-13: 978-0-7660-2240-9
ISBN-10: 0-7660-2240-4

Joan Lowery Nixon
Masterful Mystery Writer
ISBN-13: 978-0-7660-2194-5
ISBN-10: 0-7660-2194-7

Orson Scott Card
Architect of Alternate Worlds
ISBN-13: 978-0-7660-2354-3
ISBN-10: 0-7660-2354-0

Gary Paulsen
Voice of Adventure and Survival
ISBN-13: 978-0-7660-2721-3
ISBN-10: 0-7660-2721-X

Robert Cormier
Author of The Chocolate War
ISBN-13: 978-0-7660-2719-0
ISBN-10: 0-7660-2719-8

Philip Pullman
Master of Fantasy
ISBN-13: 978-0-7660-2447-2
ISBN-10: 0-7660-2447-4

Roald Dahl
Author of Charlie and the Chocolate Factory
ISBN-13: 978-0-7660-2353-6
ISBN-10: 0-7660-2353-2

R. L. Stine
Creator of Creepy and Spooky Stories
ISBN-13: 978-0-7660-2445-8
ISBN-10: 0-7660-2445-8

Paula Danziger
Voice of Teen Troubles
ISBN-13: 978-0-7660-2444-1
ISBN-10: 0-7660-2444-X

J. R. R. Tolkien
Master of Imaginary Worlds
ISBN-13: 978-0-7660-2246-1
ISBN-10: 0-7660-2246-3

C. S. Lewis
Chronicler of Narnia
ISBN-13: 978-0-7660-2446-5
ISBN-10: 0-7660-2446-6

E. B. White
Spinner of Webs and Tales
ISBN-13: 978-0-7660-2350-5
ISBN-10: 0-7660-2350-8

AUTHORS TEENS LOVE

Jerry Spinelli

Master Teller of Teen Tales

John Micklos, Jr.

Enslow Publishers, Inc.
40 Industrial Road
Box 398
Berkeley Heights, NJ 07922
USA

http://www.enslow.com

Library of Congress Cataloging-in-Publication Data

Micklos, John.
    Jerry Spinelli : master teller of teen tales / John Micklos, Jr.
        p. cm. — (Authors teens love)
    Includes bibliographical references and index.
    ISBN-13: 978-0-7660-2718-3
    ISBN-10: 0-7660-2718-X
    1. Spinelli, Jerry—Juvenile literature. 2. Authors, American—20th cen-
tury—Biography—Juvenile literature. 3. Young adult fiction—Authorship—
Juvenile literature. I. Title.
    PS3569.P546Z785 2006
    813'.54—dc22
    [B]
                                                    2006018300

Printed in the United States of America

10 9 8 7 6 5 4 3 2 1

To Our Readers: We have done our best to make sure all Internet addresses in
this book were active and appropriate when we went to press. However, the
author and publisher have no control over and assume no liability for the material available on those Internet sites or on other Web sites they may link to. Any
comments or suggestions can be sent by e-mail to comments@enslow.com or to
the address on the back cover.

Illustration Credits: Photo by Molly Thompson, courtesy of Jerry
Spinelli, p. 6; Photo by Elaine Adams, courtesy of Jerry Spinelli, p. 46;
Photos by John Micklos, Jr., pp. 67, 74; all other images courtesy of
Jerry Spinelli.

Cover Illustration: Background illustration by Mark A. Hicks; fore-
ground photo by Molly Thompson, courtesy of Jerry Spinelli.

Contents

Chapter 1

A Writing Career Begins

A goal-line stand. It all began with a goal-line stand on October 11, 1957. Norristown High School's football team led powerful Lower Merion 7–6 in the fourth quarter. But Lower Merion had the ball first and goal on Norristown's one-yard line. Lower Merion had won 32 straight games. In fact, they had not lost in three years. It seemed certain they would win this time, too.

All that stood between Lower Merion and victory was one yard. Three feet. Thirty-six inches. It seemed that only a miracle could save the game for Norristown.

In the stands, the Norristown fans held their breath. Among those fans was sixteen-year-old Jerry Spinelli. Three times a Lower Merion back ran the ball into the line. Three times the defense stopped him short of the end zone. Then came fourth down. Once again the Lower Merion back charged toward the goal line. Once again the defense held firm.

The Norristown fans erupted in cheers. Jerry cheered, too. He later recalled that long after the game ended, "at home in my room I could hear the blaring horns, the shrieks of victory."[1]

Jerry replayed the goal-line stand in his head over and over again before he went to sleep that night. He did it again in the morning. But he felt something was missing. He felt he somehow would not be satisfied until he had captured the memory in writing.

He sat at his desk and wrote down a title, "Goal to Go." The words kept flowing. Soon he had a poem:

The score stood 7–6
With but five minutes left to go.
The Ace attack employed all tricks
To settle down its stubborn foe.

It looked as though the game was done
When an Ace stepped wide 'round right.
An Eagle stopped him on the one
And tumult filled the night.

Thirty-two had come their way
And thirty-two had died.
Would number thirty-three this day
For one yard be denied?

Roy Kent, the Eagle mentor, said,
"I've waited for this game,
And now, defense, go, stop 'em dead,
And crash the Hall of Fame."

The first Ace bolted for the goal
And nothing did he see
But Branca, swearing on his soul,
"You shall not pass by me."

The next two plays convinced all
The ref would make the touchdown sign,
But when the light shone on the ball
It still lay inches from the line.

Said Captain Eastwood to his gents,
"It's up to us to stop this drive."
Said Duckworth, Avery, Knerr, and Spence,
"Will do, as long as we're alive."

The halfback drove with all his might,
His legs were jet-propelled,
But when the dust had cleared the fight,
The Eagle line had held.[2]

Jerry gave the poem to his father and forgot about it. His father thought the poem was great, and he sent it to the Norristown *Times Herald*. Several days later it appeared in the newspaper with the headline "Student Waxes Poetic." At school, everyone praised the poem.

"That, I believe, was the beginning," Jerry recalled later. From that point on, he knew he wanted to be a writer.[3]

It was not easy, though. Jerry Spinelli would endure years of waiting and hundreds of rejections before achieving success writing books. Once he broke through, however, he launched a career that made him one of the most popular authors of his generation among young readers.

Spinelli says his books are not directed just toward young people, though. "I don't write *for* kids," he says. "I write *about* kids. I write *for* everybody." Still, young readers find his books irresistible, as do teachers, librarians, and many other adult readers.[4]

Today, Spinelli still manages to maintain a young person's perspective. He does so by drawing upon memories of his own childhood. These memories lead to characters, scenes, and settings that young readers of today can still relate to.

He recalls getting a letter a few years ago from a boy who identified strongly with the character of Jason in *Space Station Seventh Grade*. "It's just like what happened to me," the boy wrote. "How do you do it?" The youngster might be shocked to learn that Jason is largely based on Jerry at age thirteen in 1954. "To me, it says that kids don't change inwardly," Spinelli says. "A thirteen-year-old is still a thirteen-year-old."[5]

Chapter 2

Making Memories

What are some of your favorite memories? Baseball games? A favorite teddy bear? Climbing trees in your backyard? We all have memories like this. Newbery Medal–winning author Jerry Spinelli takes his childhood memories and weaves them into stories that capture the universal flavor of youth.

"Our experiences as a kid are still up there in the attic of our minds—getting dusty maybe, but they're still there," Spinelli says. "My best source material is my own memory."[1]

And Spinelli, who was born February 1, 1941, to Louis Anthony Spinelli and Lorna Mae Bigler, has many memories of growing up in a middle-class neighborhood in Norristown, Pennsylvania. Some of his earliest memories involve sounds and smells. A preschooler during World War II, he recalls being frightened by the screeching wail of sirens during air raid drills. Behind his family's second-floor apartment in a row house on Marshall Street in the East End of town stood a brewery, and he also remembers how the smell of beer brewing hung over the street.[2]

Later on, there were other houses. First the family moved to a rented row house on Chestnut Street, right next to his grandparents. Then, when Jerry was in first grade, they moved to 802 George Street in the West End of town. This was the house he remembers most, the one that served as his base for playing with friends, going to school, going to church, and family times with his parents and his little brother, Bill. And, finally, there was the house on Locust Street in the North End of town, where the family moved when Jerry was in tenth grade.

He also remembers family times such as Christmas, when his parents spent very little on themselves so that Jerry and Bill could have more presents. Often there were special gifts—one year a set of Lincoln Logs, another year an even bigger surprise. That year the family had finished opening its presents from under the tree. Jerry's father commented that it had been a good year for gifts. Then someone sent Jerry into the kitchen for something, "and there it was, in front of the sink: a spanking-new cream and green whitewall-tired Roadmaster bicycle."[3]

Growing up, Jerry enjoyed Sunday dinners

Jerry Spinelli at age four in February 1945.

spent around the table at his grandparents' home. He remembers the stories of how his grandfather, Alessandro "Alex" Spinelli, crossed the Atlantic Ocean from Italy on a passenger ship all by himself at the age of fourteen. Alex spent many years as a laborer, working first for the Pennsylvania Department of Highways and later as a street sweeper in Norristown. And, as a child, Jerry heard the story of how his father, a printer, saw his mother at a dance one night at the Orioles Lodge in 1933. "See that girl," Lou Spinelli told a friend. "That's who I'm going to marry." Three years later, they did get married.[4]

But most of all, even today, Jerry Spinelli remembers the thousand details of "kidhood"— details that find their way into many of his books. These details ring as true with young readers today as they did during his own youth. They give his books a richness and depth that stand as hallmarks of his work.

Jerry's early activities as a child gave no evidence that he would grow up to be a famous writer. He says he grew up as pretty much a non-reader and non-writer, although he does recall fond memories of his mother reading *Babar the Elephant* to him when he was little.[5]

"Except for schoolwork, about the only things I read were sports pages and the backs of cereal boxes," he says. "I regret that now. I wish I could go back and change it, but I can't. The best I can do is have one of my characters [Maniac Magee] carry a book everywhere he goes. It's the closest

I can come to going back in time and doing it right."[6]

Jerry did read comic books—Bugs Bunny and cowboy and war comics. As he got older, he also read the sports pages of the Norristown *Times Herald* (where his football poem would later be published). But not real books. Hardly ever real books. "I read maybe ten of them, fifteen tops, from the day I entered first grade until graduation from high school," he says.[7]

"When I did read, I enjoyed it," he recalls, "but when I thought about how to spend my spare time, reading didn't usually come to mind. Baseball, football, and basketball did."[8]

But he did like words. Jerry loved word play and jokes that depended on funny wording twists. He enjoyed looking at the definitions of interesting words in the dictionary. And he was an excellent speller. In sixth grade, he represented his school in the county spelling bee. He lasted until the fourth round, when he misspelled "lacquer."[9]

Still, the only writing he remembers from those early years involved a poem he wrote in sixth grade as part of a project to create a scrapbook of Mexico. He gathered pictures of Mexico and then, as something extra, he wrote a three-stanza poem that ended with a touristy appeal: "Now, isn't that where you would like to be?"[10]

The poem must have been good. In fact, it was so good that his teacher did not believe he had written it himself. She thought he must have copied it from somewhere. His mother had to meet with the teacher and explain that it was his original work. Still, despite this talent for writing, five years passed before he wrote his next poem.

His growing-up years may not have included a lot of reading and writing, but they prepared him for his career in ways he did not realize until much later. The memories he was gathering later found their way into many of his books. "Each of us, in our kidhood," he later recalled, "was a Huckleberry Finn, drifting on a current that seemed tortuously slow at times, poling for the shore to check out every slightest glimmer in the trees . . . the taste of Brussels sprouts . . . your first forward roll . . . cruising a mall without a parent . . . overnighting it . . . making your own grilled cheese sandwich . . . the thousand landfalls of our adolescence . . . And now we know what we didn't know then: What an adventure it was."[11]

In fact, Spinelli later summed up his growing-up years this way: "The first fifteen years of my life turned out to be one big research project. I thought I was simply growing up in Norristown, Pennsylvania; looking back now I can see that I was also gathering material that would one day find its way into my books."[12]

As a child, Jerry never dreamed he would one day become a famous writer. First he wanted to be a cowboy. Soon, however, his interests began to revolve around sports. His father was a ticket collector for football games and a scorekeeper for basketball games at Norristown High School. Jerry often went with him and soon developed an interest in many sports.

But Jerry's favorite sport was baseball. In fact, baseball played an important part in his life from a very young age. To help Jerry learn to bat, his dad sawed off a standard Louisville Slugger bat to seventeen inches. Then he lobbed pitches to his young son. "I regularly whacked them over the back fence into the landlady's yard," Jerry later recalled in his autobiography, *Knots in My Yo-yo String*. She lived next door, and the neighborhood kids said she was mean. "My father, according to Marshall Street lore, was the only person ever to return alive from her yard, ball in hand," he later wrote.[13]

Baseball continued to be a major part of Jerry's life throughout his growing up years. He dreamed of being a professional baseball shortstop—preferably for the New York Yankees. At age thirteen, his Knee-Hi team (for ages 13–15, following Little League) won the state championship. He earned a large trophy and a jacket saying "State Champions."[14]

He continued to play baseball into high school, but he never learned to hit a curve ball. He realized that his dream of playing shortstop in the major leagues would never come true. But he continued to love the game.

Jerry excelled at other sports, too. In elementary school, he won the 50-yard dash in a contest that involved all the Norristown grade schools. "My memory of those fifty yards has nothing to do with sprinting but with two sensations," he later

A twelve-year-old Jerry Spinelli in his baseball uniform. Spinelli was shortstop for the Exchange Club Little League Green Sox.

recalled. "The first was surprise that I could not see any other runners. This led to a startling conclusion: *I must be ahead!* Which led to the second sensation: an anxious expectation, a waiting to be overtaken. I never was. I won."[15]

Jerry was also a good student, both in terms of the grades he earned and in terms of his behavior. His teachers liked and respected him. Indeed, he was successful at almost everything he did—at least through junior high school.

His success peaked in ninth grade. He won the election for student body president. He had a steady girlfriend, pretty Judy Pierson. In fact, at the ninth-grade prom, he was named king and Judy was named queen. Their picture appeared in the Norristown *Times Herald* the following week. He also delivered the valedictory speech at the Stewart Junior High School graduation on June 19, 1956.

Things changed, however, when he entered Norristown High School. He went from being a big-shot to being a nobody. He lost the election for class president. Classes grew harder. He could not make the varsity baseball team. His beloved dog, Lucky, was hit and killed by a car. The family's new home on Locust Street just did not seem the same as his old home.

In short, nothing seemed quite right any more. His old dreams were fading. And then came the football poem that started him on the road toward a new dream.

Chapter 3

If at First You Don't Succeed

The publication of the football poem that set Jerry Spinelli on a new career path came at a perfect time. "My dream of becoming a major-league baseball player was fading," he later recalled.

> The imperative to find my course in life was upon me. I was shopping around for who I wanted to be. And here this writing thing seemed to reach down and pluck me out of the crowd. I mean, it wasn't forced, it wasn't planned. Nobody assigned me to write a poem after the game. I didn't try to get it published. I didn't seek the resulting notoriety. All this pretty much just happened to me. What I did was just apply a little common sense: I like to write, I seem to be pretty good at it, people seem to like what I write (admittedly a lot to conclude from a single poem)—ergo, I'll be a writer. Simple![1]

In fact, Spinelli's path to becoming a full-time professional writer proved to be anything but simple. After high school, he attended Gettysburg College in Gettysburg, Pennsylvania, about 100 miles from his home in Norristown. He majored in English. "I would've liked to major in writing, but they didn't offer a major in that," he said.[2]

Spinelli did, however, take two writing courses from Kathrine Kressmann Taylor, who had written a best-selling book a number of years earlier. He enjoyed her class and considered her a mentor.

Spinelli told his freshman advisor in college that he was going to be a writer, and he recalled that the advisor gave him a "kindly little smile as if he knew a secret he wasn't telling me. It wasn't until years later that I understood what was behind that smile—that it's one thing to make such a statement and another thing to accomplish it," he said.[3]

After graduating from Gettysburg College in 1963, Spinelli went on to do graduate studies at the Johns Hopkins University in Baltimore, Maryland. He earned a master's degree in the Writing Seminars program there. His thesis consisted of the four short stories he wrote that year.

After finishing graduate school in 1965, Spinelli joined the Naval Air Reserve. He went to boot camp in Memphis, Tennessee, and then to photographic intelligence school in Denver, Colorado. He remained in the reserves until 1972.

In the winter of 1966, he got his first full-time job with Chilton Company, serving as a menswear and sporting goods editor for a magazine that was distributed to department stores. It was an exciting job—too exciting for Spinelli. He wanted a job where he could go home at the end of the day and not think about work any more. He wanted to have his hours outside of work free for writing.

So he found a job on a magazine called *Product Design and Development* that went to design engineers. "I told the secretary I was writing a book so I would only be there for a year or two," Spinelli later recalled. Little did he realize that two years would turn into more than two decades.[4]

Spinelli stayed with Chilton Company for twenty-three years, writing during his lunch hours, evenings, and weekends. Every day on his lunch hour, he would close his office door and craft novels using yellow magazine copy paper.[5]

He spent three years writing his first novel. He sent it out to many different publishers, but nobody wanted it. Then he wrote another novel. Nobody wanted that either. In fact, over a period of fifteen years, he wrote four unpublished novels. Still he kept plugging away. "I was saying 'just do it' to myself long before Nike made it a worldwide slogan," he said. "When I finished one book nobody wanted, I just started another one."[6]

One of his unpublished books was called *The Shoe*. He titled another *The End of the Golden Bears*. A third was called *The Corn Goddess*. "I forget what the other one was called—mercifully," he said.[7]

Still, life was good. In 1966 Spinelli met a pretty

lady named Eileen Mesi at his work. "I first became aware of Eileen's presence in the world when I came in to work one day and found a chocolate Easter bunny on my desk," he recalled.[8]

In fact, Eileen was constantly doing kindly and sometimes quirky good deeds for people. Years later, she became the model for Spinelli's Stargirl character.

Some time after receiving the chocolate bunny, Spinelli bumped into Eileen at a trolley stop. Like him, she was an aspiring writer. She dropped several binders of poetry onto his lap as he sat on the bench waiting for the trolley. Startled, he began to read them. "Very nice. This is nice," was all he could say.[9]

"Perhaps I was unfair to her since I saw her as Eileen in the circulation department," Spinelli said. "After all, how good of a poet could she be? That compromised my judgment; I only saw half of what was there, and my compliments were half empty. Still, if I'd had my wits I would have fallen off the bench over her right then."[10]

Soon enough, though, he did "fall off the bench" over her, and they married on May 21, 1977. Life was never dull. Eileen already had children, and money was tight. "You do things differently when there are kids involved," Spinelli said. "If it were just the two of us, we could've lived on beans in an apartment." Instead, they cut corners wherever they could. "For years, that's how we survived—on thrift shops, yard sales, and double coupons."[11]

During that time, Spinelli kept writing whenever there was a quiet moment. Those moments were rare. "I even sent away for a gizmo that makes ocean sounds to cover background noise, but there's no surf that's a match for six kids in the house," he later recalled.[12]

Still he managed to keep writing. And still the rejections kept coming. Now he is able to make light of it, but at the time it really hurt. "People tend to think when you're a published writer and you talk about rejection that you have a really thick skin and you're strong. I was just as devastated by the rejection slips as anyone else would be. Every one of the hundreds and hundreds broke my heart and made me feel like a rotten failure," he said.[13]

"But a funny thing happened," he added. If he got a rejection slip on a Monday, the sun still came up on Tuesday. Wednesday, the sun came up again, and he realized that the world was not ending. By Friday things were pretty nearly back to normal. "At that point, there was no reason not to get another envelope, another stamp, and send it to another publisher," he said.[14]

At a keynote speech for the Winter 2005 Society of Children's Book Writers and Illustrators meeting in New York City, Spinelli noted that over a fifteen-year period, he earned a grand total of $200 from his writing. He emptied a large bag full of rejection letters onto the podium. "These are just a few of them," he said. "Instead of rejection letters, publishers should send rejection bricks.

Decades of work should not be able to fit in an envelope. You should be able to build a house with them."[15]

During the speech, he also told the story of how one night he saw a Public Broadcasting Service (PBS) fundraiser on Channel 12. One of the items being auctioned to the highest bidder was a night on the town in New York City with bestselling author George Plimpton. At that time the Spinellis had $430 in the bank. Eileen pledged $425, and they won the evening with Plimpton. PBS sent them Plimpton's telephone number. Some months later Spinelli called Plimpton, who said he knew nothing about the arrangement. Plimpton was about to hang up, but then he asked what the winning bid was. When Spinelli told him it was $425—just $5 less than the family's savings—Plimpton said he would go.[16]

Several months later, Jerry and Eileen went to New York City to visit with Plimpton and his wife, the model Frederica. They went to Elaine's Restaurant. Many well-known authors ate there. At the first table sat Kurt Vonnegut. At the next table was Irwin Shaw. Then came the table that Plimpton had reserved. At dinner Plimpton said, "So you're a writer. I bet you'd like me to read something." Spinelli nodded. Plimpton said he would, but warned, "Don't write a book about a young boy growing up. The world doesn't need another one of those." Of course, that is exactly what Spinelli's manuscript was about.[17]

Back home, Eileen suggested that Jerry contact

Philadelphia Magazine about writing an article based on this experience. The magazine accepted the article and paid him $400—twice as much as he had made in the previous fifteen years from his writing. Things were beginning to look up. Soon they got even better. By the time the article appeared, Spinelli's first novel had been accepted for publication—a novel that had its beginning with a bag of chicken bones.

Chapter 4

Chicken Bones Bring Success at Last

One morning in 1980, Jerry Spinelli opened the refrigerator to get his lunch for work. Little did he know that what he would find (or not find) would change his writing life forever. He had packed left-over chicken. When he opened the bag, all he found were bones. One of his six children—to this day he doesn't know which one—had eaten all the meat off the bones and placed the bones back in the bag.

At lunch that day Spinelli sat down and started writing a story with that incident as its opening scene. At first he wrote it from the father's point of view. Then he decided it would be more interesting to tell the story from the viewpoint of the chicken snatcher. And thus he had the opening scene of what would become his first published book, *Space Station Seventh Grade*. In its final form, the scene reads like this:

> One by one my stepfather took the chicken bones out of the bag and laid them on the kitchen table. He laid them down real neat. In a row. Five of them. Two leg bones, two wing bones, one thigh bone.
>
> And bones is all they were. There wasn't a speck of meat on them.
>
> Was this really happening? Did my stepfather really drag me out of bed at seven o'clock in the morning on my summer vacation so I could stand in the kitchen in my underpants and stare down at a row of chicken bones?[1]

Space Station Seventh Grade describes the adventures of thirteen-year-old Jason Herkimer as he negotiates the challenges of seventh grade, including the onset of puberty, building a miniature space station, and handling first crushes. The book includes all of the uproarious and sometimes crude behavior of teenage boys. It paints a convincing portrait of the ups and downs of adolescent life.

The manuscript, too, faced many ups and downs on its road to publication. Spinelli had been trying for some time to get an agent who could help him place his work with publishers. Agents serve as editorial matchmakers. They try to place an author's books with the editors and publishers who are most likely to want them.

As Spinelli found out, though, finding an agent can be just as challenging as finding a publisher. "Many publishers won't look at unsolicited manuscripts unless they come from an agent, and many agents won't take unpublished authors," Spinelli says. This makes it hard for new authors to break into the field.[2]

After finishing three chapters of the manuscript that would become *Space Station Seventh Grade*, Spinelli wrote to Jerre Mangione, an award-winning author who taught at the University of Pennsylvania, asking for advice. Mangione suggested he contact an agent named Ray Lincoln. Spinelli did so, but Lincoln responded that she would not read the manuscript unless it was finished.

Spinelli went to work the next day dejected. It seemed that yet another roadblock stood in his way. But when he arrived home that evening Eileen was waiting. She said she had called Lincoln and persuaded her to read the three chapters. Spinelli immediately sent them to her. About a week later he received a letter complimenting his writing and saying that Lincoln would be happy to be his agent. "I'm not sure I've ever had a bigger moment in my writing life than this," he says.[3]

After nearly a quarter century of writing, Spinelli had finally gotten his big break. His confidence grew. "A professional agent in the business believed that I could sell—that a publisher would be interested in buying my manuscript," he recalls.

"That Monday, I didn't need shoes. I flew across the parking lot to work."[4]

With the incentive of knowing he had an agent to represent his manuscript, Spinelli picked up speed. He finished the book within a couple of months. Lincoln sent it to a couple of publishers, placing it with Little, Brown and Company.

Little, Brown editor John Keller later recalled his reaction to the manuscript. He liked the first chapter's "conversational, unpretentious tone." What really drew his attention, however, was a scene in Chapter 4 in which Spinelli described Jason's feelings as he stands in the shower room after gym class and notices the presence or absence of pubic hair on the other boys. "I broke into a big grin and thought, exactly!" Keller recalled. "That, I believe, is Jerry's greatest strength. He gets it right."[5]

There is also a chapter in *Space Station Seventh Grade* titled "Grandmothers." In this chapter, Jason shows his friend Peter Kim the space station he is building. The two boys discuss topics such as time, space, infinity . . . and grandmothers. Jerry says of all the chapters he has ever written, this one is his favorite.[6]

But there were still some hurdles to overcome. Little, Brown thought the manuscript was too long and asked for a revision. Also, Spinelli had prepared the book with an adult audience in mind, as he had done with his previous manuscripts. Little, Brown, however, believed the manuscript would appeal more to young adults. They thought adults wouldn't want to read about the adventures of a thirteen-year-old boy.

Little, Brown also wanted Spinelli to change the title. "I originally called it *Stuff*, and now I wish I had stuck with it," Spinelli later said. In the end, Little, Brown persuaded him to change the title to *Space Station Seventh Grade*. He preferred the original title, but most of all he wanted to get the book published.[7]

Space Station Seventh Grade came out in 1982. Readers and critics alike praised the book. Reviewer Marilyn H. Karrenbrock summed the book up in the *ALAN Review* by saying, "Here, in the tradition of Judy Blume, is a boy's book which both sexes will enjoy."[8]

Spinelli's favorite comment about the book, he said, came from Jim Trelease, author of the *Read-Aloud Handbook*, who called it the best book about adolescent boys since *Catcher in the Rye*.[9]

And so, a quarter century after his football poem had convinced him he wanted to be a writer, Jerry Spinelli published his first novel. Today, more than twenty years and twenty books later, it remains his favorite. "It was just such a thrill after all those years, and having written four books that were unpublished," he later recalled. "I was just as happy about that first book being published as I was about winning the Newbery Medal."[10]

Spinelli's ultimate goal, however, involved much more than publishing just one book.

Chapter 5

More Books and a Daring Decision

Spinelli's first book had grown naturally out of an event in his home. Where would his next topic come from? In the end, it came from the publisher. "I sent about half a dozen ideas to Little, Brown, and they picked sibling rivalry," he said.[1]

While the overall theme may have come from outside, much of the material for the book again came from Spinelli's own household. The battles between two of his children formed the basis for *Who Put That Hair in My Toothbrush?*, published by Little, Brown and Company in 1984. "From our six kids have come a number of stories," Spinelli has said. "Jeffrey and Molly, who were always fighting, have been especially helpful."[2]

The story is told by fourteen-year-old Greg Tofer

and his twelve-year-old sister, Megin, in alternate chapters. Their sibling rivalry is so intense that they even have special names for each other: Greg is "El Grosso," and Megin is "Megamouth." The book revolves around their conflicts and the event that finally manages to bring them a bit closer together.

Of all his books, Spinelli thinks *Who Put That Hair in My Toothbrush?* was the hardest to write because the chapters alternate between Greg's and Megin's point of view. "It was hard to figure out how to keep the story moving when it was being told from two different points of view," Spinelli said.[3]

> "I do enjoy the challenge of being someone I'm not."
> —Jerry Spinelli

Yet he found the book gratifying as well. Indeed, he sees Megin Tofer as one of the favorite characters he has ever created, partly because she is so feisty. Asked if it is hard to write from a girl's perspective, Spinelli replied, "I'm not sure I feel that it is. I do enjoy the challenge of being someone I'm not. To some extent that's what drives authors and actors—the chance to be someone you're not."[4]

Spinelli was not the only one who liked the characters and action in *Who Put That Hair in My Toothbrush?* Reviewers and readers also accepted the book warmly. "The book accurately depicts adolescent travails and the fierce battles that often erupt within other families," wrote Judy Rowen.[5]

"The nasty (though not dangerous) lengths to

which they [Megin and Greg] carry their constant sibling rivalry will provoke laughs, gasps, and possibly admiration from readers who have pulled similar pranks," noted reviewer Barbara J. Craig in *ALAN Reviews*. "Middle-school readers, male and female, will enjoy this well-written, fast-paced novel whose characters come alive from the first moment we meet them."[6]

Spinelli's third book, *Jason and Marceline*, published in 1986, revisited Jason Herkimer and his former nemesis (and now girlfriend) Marceline as they make their way through their ninth grade year. This book also proved popular. Reviewer Gloria Miklowitz wrote an article in the *Los*

> ## "Spinelli captures perfectly the adolescent boy. . . . It's a book kids . . . will love."
> —Gloria Miklowitz

Angeles Times that summed it up this way: "Spinelli captures perfectly the adolescent boy who supposedly has a sexual thought every seven seconds. It's a book kids of either sex—from sixth grade though ninth—will love."[7]

Spinelli followed this book with *Night of the Whale*, which told the story of an aspiring writer named Mouse Umlau who shares a beachside vacation with some friends. The rowdy high school seniors devote themselves to partying until the night they encounter a group of beached whales.

This book appeared in 1985, again published by Little, Brown.

His next book was *Dump Days*, which featured younger characters. In this book, published by Little, Brown in 1988, two eleven-year-old friends, Duke Pickwell and J.D. Kidd, plan a perfect summer day doing all their favorite things. The plot revolves around their schemes to get money to pay for this.

Again, the book received favorable reviews. "Spinelli spins a story that weaves together the shared conversations and small-town adventures of a friendship based on trust, humor, compassion, and imagination," said the review in *Publishers Weekly*.[8]

Dump Days was also notable for its brief mention of Maniac Magee, who would later become Spinelli's most famous character: "Maniac Magee, who's an orphan sort of kid, who sleeps at the bandshell."[9]

With five books behind him, Spinelli made a daring decision. He quit his job as a magazine editor in 1989 so he could write full time. "My goal had always been not to get a book published but to make my living writing fiction," he said.[10]

Few people make a living writing children's books, though. With a family to support, Spinelli knew he was taking a chance. Still, he knew he needed to make a break if he wanted his dream to come true. He thought he could do it, "if I only had the gumption to take a shot. So I quit my job of twenty-three years and launched into the unknown." And that unknown at first involved what he later described as "a shaky ride and a leaky boat."[11]

In 1990, two more of Spinelli's books appeared. *The Bathwater Gang* starred J. D. Kidd's little sister, Bertie, who organizes a kid "gang" that competes against an all-boy gang. The adventure, which Susan Hepler of *School Library Journal* described as "light and entertaining," ends in a giant mud fight and an agreement that it is better to do things together.[12]

But it was Spinelli's other book that year, *Maniac Magee*, which would change his life forever.

Chapter 6

A Marvelous Maniac

"The earliest, most specifically identifiable source for the story [of Maniac Magee] turns out to be reflected on the hardback cover: Carol Palmer's terrific photograph of the legs—jeans and sneakers—of a boy running," said Spinelli.[1] Several years earlier, a friend told Spinelli about how when he was a kid he would run everywhere rather than bike. He ran three miles to the hoagie shop or six miles to the movie theater.

Spinelli loved that image, so he tucked it away for future reference "along with the dozens, hundreds of other appealing tidbits awaiting the right setting, the right story."[2]

The idea simmered for a while and finally began to take shape. Spinelli had turned in his fifth novel and was thinking about what to write about for his sixth. He decided he wanted to write about "a hero, a kid who's a hero especially to other kids."[3] Spinelli named him Maniac after a real-life kid he had once read about in a newspaper column.

Spinelli also decided to place Maniac in an unconventional setting. Maniac was an orphan running away from everything—his home, his school, his aunt and uncle. Spinelli asked John Keller, his editor at Little, Brown, if he could write about "a kid who doesn't have a family or a home and doesn't go to school?" Keller told him to go for it.[4]

So Spinelli had a great idea and a great character. The rest would be easy, right? Wrong. Spinelli struggled with the story. He wrote eighty pages and threw them away. He started again, writing another eighty pages. Still he did not like it.[5]

The hard part was getting the right voice for telling the story. First he tried the first-person point of view, with Maniac telling his own story. But that did not work. Then he tried the "third-person, author-knows-best voice. Maniac sounded like a cardboard kid on a cereal box."[6] He tried other voices. None of them worked either.

Finally, he decided to take a break from the project. Then suddenly one evening, the opening line for the book came to him: "They say Maniac Magee was born in a dump."[7]

Spinelli now not only had the opening line, but he had the voice: "they say." The book would be about the town's collective memory of this unusual hero. "That's one time when the muse came to me,"

Spinelli said, recalling the moment. "Then I went ahead and wrote the book."[8]

The story began to take shape, but it still lacked focus. Then Spinelli had an idea for how to give it unity. "It occurred to me about then that this was my chance to say some things about people and color that had been on my mind for a long time," he said.[9]

He drew from a scene he had once written about a race between the fastest white kid and the fastest black kid in town. He remembered a girl he had once met who carried her entire home library to school each day in a suitcase. He recalled the black-white divisions in his own hometown growing up. Then he stitched it all together, with Maniac being the unlikely force that begins to bring the two groups just a little closer together.

Spinelli wrote out the draft for *Maniac Magee* longhand, making adjustments and edits along the way. Each day he read aloud what he had written the day before and made changes. In the end, he had a stack of 550 handwritten pages about 5 inches tall. He spent two weeks typing the manuscript on a manual typewriter. (These were the days before he started to use a computer for his writing.) Once he was finished typing, he did not even read the manuscript through again. At that point, he simply sent it to his publisher. "I kind of rationalized that I made changes as I typed along," he said. "As I look back, it's amazing I produced anything that made sense. To this day, I haven't read it."[10]

Jerry Spinelli poses with Kirbee Krimpet, the mascot for Maniac Magee's favorite food.

But millions of other readers have. *Maniac Magee* became an immediate hit among readers and critics alike. Here are a few of the reviewers' reactions to the book:

- *Publishers Weekly* called it a "humorous yet poignant tall tale."[11]

- "The story, which explores such complex concepts as home and race relations, is consistently fresh and surprising," said reviewer Louise Sherman in *School Library Journal*.[12]

- The book "has the tone of a story that has come down through the years," said *The New York Times Book Review*.[13]

Spinelli had no idea at the time that *Maniac Magee* would become as wildly successful as it did. He did realize, however, that he had written a special book, and he still considers it his signature work. In 2000, he recommended it as the one book of his that people should read, "for the message, the story, and the language."[14]

Awards committees loved the book, too. In the fall of 1990, *Maniac Magee* won the Boston Globe/Horn Book Award. Then in January 1991 came a call that changed Spinelli's life forever. He remembers it well. The phone rang late at night, and his first thought was, "Uh-oh. Who's dead? How often have you gotten a call late at night with good news?"[15]

This call, however, brought very good news. It was Alice Naylor, chair of the Newbery Committee.

She informed him that *Maniac Magee* had won the 1991 Newbery Medal, the highest honor in American children's literature.

Spinelli said his two youngest children were still at home at the time. One slept through the entire commotion. The other came out of his room and asked what was going on, but he did not seem very excited when he heard the news. Jerry and Eileen stayed up most of the rest of the night, though, talking about the award and what it would mean for their future.

Several hours later, they went back to bed, but they were too excited to sleep. So they went to breakfast at a local diner in Phoenixville. "We ordered bacon with our eggs," Spinelli recalled. "That was the extent of our treat."[16]

Once the honor was officially announced later that morning, the phone started ringing and flowers started arriving. "Our living room ended up full of flowers," Spinelli recalls. "It's been a parade ever since."[17]

Spinelli had been sworn not to tell anyone about the award before the official announcement, but years later he admitted, "We actually did spill the beans to our local librarian."[18]

The honor came at a good time. Money had been tight since he quit his full-time editing job. Winning the Newbery Medal virtually ensured that *Maniac Magee* would be a popular book for years to come. The award also brought renewed attention to his other books. Spinelli now knew he could make ends meet as a writer.

Chapter 7

Not Resting on His Laurels

How do you follow up a big hit? Pop singers face this dilemma all the time. So do artists and movie stars. And so do authors. With a body of work already to his credit, it was certain that Jerry Spinelli was no "one-hit wonder." And he knew he had many stories left to tell.

In fact, 1991 not only saw him win the Newbery Medal, but also saw the release of three other books with two new publishers. Until then, all of his books had been published by Little, Brown and Company. But even before the Newbery Medal, other publishers had asked him to write for them, too.

In 1991 Scholastic published two of Spinelli's books: *Fourth Grade Rats* and *Report to the*

Principal's Office. Spinelli has often said that his ideas come from lots of places—his family, his memories, and things he reads. *Fourth Grade Rats* came from a schoolyard rhyme he remembered from his childhood:

First grade babies!
Second grade cats!
Third grade angels!
Fourth grade . . . RRRRRATS![1]

One day that rhyme popped into his head, and he immediately thought, "There's a natural title of a kids' book." He started with the title and then "took a month to think of the story that went with it."[2]

The book describes how fourth grader Suds Morton, at the urging of his best friend, Joey Peterson, tries to misbehave in order to live up to the term "rat." Along the way he tries to impress pretty Judy Billings. In the end, he discovers that misbehaving is not nearly as much fun as it sounds and that maybe he can be a fourth grader without being a rat. *Fourth Grade Rats* appealed to young readers, winning the Black-Eyed Susan Award, the South Carolina Children's Book Award, and the KC3 Reading Award (greater Kansas City). It also appealed to reviewers. "Rapid-fire dialogue and a hilarious string of episodes unfold a story with a valuable message about peer pressure and the importance of being oneself," said the review in *Publishers Weekly*.[3]

Report to the Principal's Office, which focused on the adventures of middle-schoolers Sunny, Eddie, Salem, and Pickles, marked the first of a series of books featuring these characters. The books are short, funny, and easy to read. The four main characters, who at first seem unlikely friends, soon form a tight-knit group. Young readers formed a bond with the characters, too, and eagerly looked forward to their next adventures. In *School Library Journal*, reviewer Pamela K. Bomboy wrote, "Readers will recognize themselves as these feisty characters meet the challenges and find themselves actually looking forward to the next day of school."[4]

Spinelli's third book in 1991 was titled *There's a Girl in My Hammerlock* and was published by Simon & Schuster. The idea came from a newspaper article he read about a female wrestler on the school wrestling team who competed against boys. In his book, eighth grader Maisie Potter tries out for wrestling and ultimately makes the squad.

Like Megin Tofer in *Who Put That Hair in My Toothbrush?*, Maisie Potter is scrappy, independent, and a bit out of the mainstream. Spinelli thinks that makes a character interesting. "If 100 people are running north in a herd and one is running south, which one are you going to want to read about and write about?" he once said.[5]

Readers and reviewers alike agreed that *There's a Girl in My Hammerlock* was special. Reviewer Ted Hipple, writing for *ALAN Reviews*, called it "a fine novel" that brings into a focus:

Jerry Spinelli with a couple of animal friends, Chi-Chi Chinchilla and Bernie the Rat.

a number of issues related to gender matters, to sports, and the difficulties of being in eighth grade, but all with a light touch. Sometimes hilarious, sometimes poignant, often provocative, and always compelling, this work will be read with considerable pleasure by middle schoolers, boys and girls alike, those on the teams and those who follow them. And in Maisie they will find a hero/heroine/wrestler who mixes grit and charm and uncertainty and determination in just the right amounts.[6]

This book also won a number of honors, including being chosen as a Young Adult Library Services Association (YALSA) Best Book for Young Adults. It also won the California Young Reader Medal and the Charlotte Award. All in all, 1991 marked a truly spectacular year for Jerry Spinelli.

And he kept up the pace over the next few years. Through Scholastic, he published three more books about Sunny, Eddie, Salem, and Pickles. With Little, Brown, he did *The Bathwater Gang Gets Down to Business*, a sequel to *The Bathwater Gang*.

As Spinelli's career progressed, his approach to the writing process evolved. "I used to write very fastidiously, deliberately," he said. In fact, he remembers spending six weeks one time searching for a perfect metaphor. "I don't do that any more. I started to write faster once I got published. I shifted my viewpoint from fine art to performing art."[7]

Part of that philosophy also came from the realization that in order to maintain a successful career as a fiction writer he had to continue to publish new books. Still, he always keeps working on each book until he believes it is as good as he can make it. Depending on the length and complexity of the project, he may spend up to a year crafting each book, and he generally works on only one book at a time.

In 1995, Spinelli published a book titled *Tooter Pepperday* for Random House. Tooter is a feisty young girl who objects to her family's move from the city to her aunt's farm. In the end, however, she discovers that life on the farm really does have its rewards as she "babysits" an egg until it hatches. "Tooter is a real-life, plucky, resourceful heroine . . . in a good sound story that has a lot to say about the choices we make and the impact they have," said the review in *Booklist*.[8]

In 1996, *Crash* appeared, published by Knopf. Its central character, John "Crash" Coogan, at first seems to be a stereotypical jock football star—tough, crude, and mostly interested in setting the junior high school record for scoring touchdowns. In the end, however, he turns out to be much more complex than that. The story revolves around his relationship with Penn Webb, a puny Quaker vegetarian who moves to his block the summer before first grade. From then through seventh grade, Penn tries to be friends, but Crash most often responds by picking on him.

When Crash's grandfather suffers a stroke, he begins to reevaluate what is truly important in life. And when Penn finally beats him in a race after years of trying, Crash finds himself happy for Penn rather than resentful. By the end of the book,

Penn is Crash's best friend rather than the object of his ridicule.

Reviewers praised *Crash* for its well-rounded treatment of a character who is basically a bully. "Without being preachy, Spinelli packs a powerful moral wallop, leaving it to the pitch-perfect narration to drive home his point," said a review in *Publishers Weekly*.[9]

"Readers will devour this humorous glimpse at what jocks are made of while learning that life does not require crashing helmet-headed through it," wrote Connie Tyrrell Burns in *School Library Journal*.[10]

Other reviewers pointed out how few books had taken this approach in dealing with the subject of bullies. Spinelli, who reads very few books for young readers (and does not even read his own once they have been published), found that surprising. "Reviewers surprised me by noting the rarity if not uniqueness of a story told from a bully's point of view; I'd have thought there were many such books," he said.[11]

Crash won many honors, including being named a Best Book of the Year by *School Library Journal*. In addition, young readers in eleven states voted *Crash* as their favorite book of the year. The book also was named to the International Reading Association's Children's Choices list, which reflects the opinions of young readers across the United States.[12]

In 1997, Scholastic published a special book they had asked Spinelli to write. *The Library Card* included four stories with different characters, all loosely connected by a blue library card that somehow affects their lives. One story features a character nicknamed Mongoose, which was inspired by Spinelli's longstanding interest in nicknames. This dated back to his school days, when his nickname was Spit—a not very flattering derivative from Spinelli. "Other people had really neat nicknames, and here I was called Spit," he recalled.[13]

Spinelli was pleased with how *The Library Card* turned out. He remembered what he had missed by not being a reader growing up, and he enjoyed writing a book that encouraged youngsters to explore the wonder of reading.

Others liked *The Library Card*, too. "Spinelli has created stories that touch both the heart and funny bone," wrote reviewer Mary Sue Preissner.[14] "Spinelli is a shrewd storyteller, balancing lighter moments with provocative ones to meaningful effect," said a reviewer in *Kirkus Reviews*.[15]

That same year marked the publication of *Wringer* by HarperCollins, another book inspired by the newspaper. For years, Spinelli had read articles about a small Pennsylvania town that raised money by having an annual event that revolves around people paying to shoot pigeons in a giant field. He thought it seemed an interesting situation for a book, but for a long time he could not put a story with it.

Then one year he read about young boys who served as wringers. Their job was to wring the necks of pigeons who were injured but not killed by the gunfire. At that point, the story became clear. "How about writing the story from one of these kids' points of view?" he thought. "In a town where every boy is expected to become a wringer on his 10th birthday, what happens to a boy who doesn't want to be a wringer?"[16]

With this premise, Spinelli wove a compelling tale about young Palmer LaRue's dilemma as he faces the prospect of being a wringer. To further complicate matters, Palmer befriends a pigeon that becomes his pet. In the end, he decides not to be a wringer, despite the ridicule he knows he will endure. "The story moves at a fast pace and the tension never lets up," said reviewer Marilyn Courtot on the Children's Literature website. "Palmer's final epiphany is a welcome relief."[17]

Other critics agreed. The review on Amazon.com said, "*Wringer* will appeal to preteens and younger teens who love to read suspenseful books on their own, but it would also be a good story to read aloud to spark discussion about the perils and nuances of peer pressure."[18]

Wringer also scored with awards committees. It was named a Newbery Honor Book in 1998. In addition, the book won The Carolyn Field Award and the Josette Frank Award. After all his success with these fiction projects, however, Spinelli's next project took him in an entirely different direction.

Chapter 8

Talking About the Memories

One of the things that makes Jerry Spinelli's books special is his inclusion of descriptions of childhood based on his own memories of growing up in Norristown, Pennsylvania. These descriptions ring as true with readers today as they did when the events were happening fifty years ago.

Spinelli's next project took him back to those days through a book titled *Knots in My Yo-yo String* (subtitled *The Autobiography of a Kid*), which was published by Knopf in 1998. The book takes him from birth to high school, with an emphasis on the elementary and junior high school years.

Alert readers will find references to many

incidents that later find their way into his books. Here are just a few:

- In fifth grade he won the 50-yard dash championship among all elementary schools in Norristown. Races figure prominently in *Maniac Magee*, *Crash*, and *Loser*.

- As a youngster, Jerry marveled at the nighttime sky. Jason Herkimer does the same thing in *Space Station Seventh Grade*.

- As a child, Jerry prided himself on neatness and was upset to constantly find knots in his yo-yo string. *Maniac Magee* adds to his status as a legend by unraveling a knot that no one else had ever untied.

- In elementary school, Jerry had a girlfriend named Judy Brooks. In *Fourth Grade Rats*, Suds Morton likes a girl named Judy Billings.

- Jerry's interest in and concern about race relations as a youngster turns up as a unifying theme in *Maniac Magee*.

Even more than specific incidents, however, it is the sights, sounds, tastes, and smells from childhood that find their way into Spinelli's books. Those details add richness and realism to his work.

Spinelli's books generally create a vivid sense of place. Much of that, too, is based on his keen recollections of his childhood hometown. Norristown became Two Mills in *Maniac Magee*.

His West End home on George Street became a home on Oriole Street in a couple of his books.

He once summarized his thoughts about his neighborhood this way:

> The West End was alleyways and brick sidewalks and sewer drains that went halfway to China. It was the red hills and the spear field and the dump, or, as the rats knew it, the playground. It was grocery stores on every other corner and Haws Avenue where the beautiful platinum blonde, Dovie Wilmoth, lived, and Stony Creek, where I explored for endless hours, rousting the crayfish from their underwater rocks. I drew a map of the West End for my novel *Dump Days*.[1]

The part Spinelli's childhood memories play in his books is perhaps best summed up in the final chapter of *Knots in My Yo-yo String*. There he describes a visit to a school in Fargo, North Dakota, in September 1992. During a question-and-answer session, a youngster asked him if he thought being a kid helped him to become a writer. The question brought back a rush of memories.

"I could have taken days to answer the boy's question," Spinelli wrote in *Knots in My Yo-yo String*, "but neither he nor Fargo had that time. So I simply nodded and smiled and said, 'Yes, I believe it did.'"[2]

Indeed, many of his childhood memories ended up appearing decades later in his books. "Ideas come from ordinary, everyday life," he once said. "And from imagination. And from feelings. And from memories. Memories of dust in my sneakers

Jerry Spinelli and his dog, Lucky, in May 1953. Childhood
memories play a huge part in Spinelli's fiction.

and humming whitewalls down a hill called Monkey."[3]

Spinelli's fans, both young readers and adults, responded well to *Knots in My Yo-yo String*. One reviewer noted: "His descriptions of his childhood universe (which does not extend beyond Norristown, Pennsylvania) elicits the use of all the five senses. . . . As Spinelli effortlessly spins the story of an ordinary Pennsylvania boy, he also documents the evolution of an exceptional author."[4]

Spinelli also had another book published in 1998. Random House published *Blue Ribbon Blues*, a sequel to *Tooter Pepperday*. In *Blue Ribbon Blues*, Tooter prepares a goat for showing at the county fair. Tooter Pepperday is an interesting character, feisty and funny. Spinelli's next project, however, would star an even more fascinating young woman in a book idea that had been bouncing around in his head for more than thirty years.

Chapter 9

A Stargirl and a Boy Called Loser

Imagine a book that took thirty-four years to write. Jerry Spinelli said he first had the idea for *Stargirl* in 1966. The book would revolve around a character who was different from other kids. At the time, he imagined the main character being a boy and thought the thing that made him different was that he lived underground. "That's how it started," Spinelli recalls. "Over the years it morphed and evolved."[1]

Those were the days of deep tensions between the United States and the Soviet Union, and many people built bomb shelters in their backyards in case a nuclear war began. So he next thought of placing a girl in a bomb shelter. At that point, he planned to call the book *Under the Bomb*. Over the years, the idea went through one phase after another. In the end, the story focused on a most unconventional young woman in the conventional setting of a typical high school. "In its final form the story finds its most specific inspiration in my wife, Eileen, some of whose good deeds . . . I happily confiscated," he said.[2]

"With all of that," Spinelli noted, "it was fairly late in the game that I decided to tell the story through a boy's eyes as a self-appointed historian/observer." Having decided that, he plucked Leo Borlock, a minor character from *Who Put That Hair in My Toothbrush?*, to tell the story.[3]

Spinelli likes to thread certain characters or themes through several of his books. "It's personally appealing to me," he said. "It gives me a sense that my work is a whole." He also liked the idea of giving Leo a bigger role to play in one of his books.[4]

Stargirl Caraway is simply not like the other students at Mica Area High School in Arizona. She plays the ukulele at lunch and sings "Happy Birthday" to people. She carries a pet rat with her. She wears unusual clothing: a 1920s flapper dress, an Indian buckskin, a kimono. When she cheers at basketball games, she cheers for *both* teams.

Nobody at school can figure her out. Within a few short months, she goes from being just a curiosity to being the most intriguing and admired girl in school to being despised—an outcast. Meanwhile, she and Leo become girlfriend and boyfriend. He shares in the isolation when she is shunned by other students.

At one point, Stargirl tries to be "normal." She dresses in jeans and sandals and goes by her given name—Susan. For a while, she tries to fit in, but still the other students do not accept her. When she returns after winning the state oratorical contest, only three people are at the school to greet her: two teachers and one student.

So she goes back to being Stargirl, living life her way and not worrying about what others think. When Leo does not invite her to the spring ball, she goes with her friend Dori Dilson, dressed in a buttercup gown. She ends up leading a bunny hop dance that involves almost all the students, and then, at the end of the evening, she simply disappears. Her family suddenly moves away, and no one ever sees her again.

Critics and readers alike loved *Stargirl*, which was published by Knopf in 2000. In addition to being a *New York Times* bestseller, the book won a Parents' Choice Gold Award and was named one of the American Library Association's Top Ten Best Books for Young Adults that year. It also won a Charlotte Award and other readers' choice awards. Barnes and Noble even came out with a *Stargirl* gift card in 2005. *Kirkus Reviews* gave the book a starred review, calling it "a magical and heartbreaking tale," and the *New York Times* said, "Spinelli has produced a poetic allegorical tale about the magnificence and rarity of true nonconformity."[5]

Stargirl also made a splash on the international

level. To date, the book has been published in more than thirty-five languages. Yet despite all the accolades for *Stargirl*, some readers questioned whether the title character was too unusual to be believable. Could a girl such as Stargirl really exist? Spinelli answered the question by saying that while he drew aspects of Stargirl from many sources, "the one person who embodies more of those aspects than anyone else I know is my wife and fellow author, Eileen."[6]

Spinelli went on to say, "Stargirl is as real as hope, as real as possibility, as real as the best in human nature. Outrageous? I hope so. Thank goodness for the outrageous among us."[7]

Perhaps the most remarkable tribute to Stargirl is the emergence of Stargirl Societies. These are groups of middle school and high school girls who find inspiration and guidance in the spirit and deeds of the character. For example, they may do things such as dropping change on the sidewalk for others to find and placing uplifting notes on people's lockers.

Spinelli's next book, *Loser*, which was published in 2002 by HarperCollins, dealt with a character who was totally different in nature. Whereas Stargirl always seems to be the center of attention, Donald Zinkoff lives life at the fringes. Donald is different, and as we follow his journey through elementary school and into middle school, those differences gradually accumulate in the eyes of his classmates until he becomes somewhat of an outsider.

Zinkoff earns the nickname "Loser" in fourth grade at Field Day. His Purple team is leading going into the final event—a relay race. He is running anchor. The team's best runner, Gary Hobin, gives him a huge lead. But here's what happens:

> Zinkoff runs and runs, the flap of his headband bobbing behind like a tiny purple tail, and he is still running long after the others have crossed the finish line. Zinkoff comes in dead last. The Purples come in last. The Purples lose the championship.
>
> The Purples tear off their headbands. They slam them to the ground, stomp them into the yellow dust. Zinkoff is bent over, gasping from his great effort, catching his breath. Hobin comes to him. He kicks dust over Zinkoff's sneakers. Zinkoff looks up. Hobin sneers, "You're a loser. A stinkin' loser."[8]

Another time, Zinkoff goes off into a snowstorm searching for a little girl who is missing. He searches for hours until he himself ends up needing to be rescued. The little girl, meanwhile, had been found soon after she disappeared.

The book ends with Zinkoff waiting to be chosen for a pick-up game of football. The sides are even, and Zinkoff is left unchosen, as always. But he does not go away. He simply stares at the team captains, waiting. Finally, grudgingly, one of them points to him and calls his name. In the end, Zinkoff is rewarded for his persistence—just as his creator, Jerry Spinelli, was when he kept plugging away waiting for his first book to be accepted.

"I would hope that the reader comes to realize that the title is ironic," Spinelli said. "Zinkoff, in spite of his bumbling, is in fact not a loser at all. 'Loser' is what others call him, not what he is."[9]

In a separate interview, Spinelli said, "Everyone loses from time to time, but that's not the same as being a 'loser.' As Zinkoff shows, the only person who can make a 'loser' out of you is yourself."[10]

Loser won numerous awards, including the Dorothy Canfield Fisher Award, the M. Jerry Weiss Book Award from the New Jersey Reading Association, and the Judy Lopez Memorial Award from the Women's National Book Association. The book also won awards from young readers in several states.

And perhaps the book will gently remind readers to think about how they treat others. "By creating such an unusually good-natured protagonist, Spinelli can show the ugly, cruel behavior of other children without making Zinkoff a pathetic victim," said a reviewer in *Publishers Weekly*. "This tack may well encourage listeners to consider how they treat their friends, classmates, and teammates."[11]

Chapter 10

Milkweed, Movies, and More

Jerry Spinelli's next two projects were about as different as two projects can be. One, titled *My Daddy and Me*, marked the first picture book of Spinelli's career. Published in 2003 by Knopf, it describes the things a little boy and his dad do together over the course of a day. Light-hearted and colorful illustrations by Seymour Chwast portray a doggy daddy and his doggy son having fun together.

Jerry's wife, Eileen Spinelli, is herself a noted poet and award-winning picture book author. Indeed, *My Daddy and Me* was inspired by Eileen's book, *When Mama Comes Home Tonight*, which was published by Simon & Schuster in 1998.

The editor of that book suggested a companion book about daddies that Jerry would write.

For a variety of reasons, the book ended up being published by Knopf instead. "It was something of an achievement in that I've been writing picture books for twenty-five years, and this is the first one that got published," he said.[1]

How did fans and critics react to this new endeavor? While the preteen and teenage readers who make up the core audience for most of his books may have found *My Daddy and Me* too "young" for them, young children and their parents responded enthusiastically.

Reviewers, too, applauded the book. "Young children will surely be comforted by this warm, simple tribute to Dadkind," wrote Karin Snelson in an Amazon.com review.[2] Meanwhile, in a review for *School Library Journal,* Leslie Barban called it "an appealing read-aloud."[3]

From the bouncy joy of a day with daddy, Spinelli's other book published in 2003 by Knopf, *Milkweed*, went in the opposite direction. It tells the dark story of a young orphan boy living on the streets of Nazi-occupied Warsaw, Poland, during World War II. Spinelli had been reading about that time period and about Holocaust survivors for years, but it was Eileen who put the idea for a specific book into his head. She told him about an article she had read about a father who gave his daughter a pill that made her seem to be dead. Then he smuggled her out of the ghetto in a coffin. "Although Spinelli didn't use the incident in the novel, the idea was his starting point," wrote Jane C. McFann in an article about how the Spinellis support each other as writers.[4]

While most of Jerry Spinelli's books are based on "a little research and a lot of imagination," *Milkweed* required a different approach. He brought home a load of books from a local bookstore and spent the next three or four months doing research. "I did more research for *Milkweed* than any other book," he said.[5]

But finally he had all the information he needed. With every book, he says, there comes a point where the researching and thinking and planning end and the actual writing begins. And so it was with *Milkweed*.[6]

Milkweed tells the story of a young orphan boy with no name who struggles to survive as the Nazis occupy Warsaw. He may have no name, but he is called many things: thief, Jew, Gypsy. He eventually is given the name Misha Pilsudski, and he moves in with the family of his friend Janina in the newly created ghetto. At night he slips through holes in the ghetto wall to smuggle in food. He escapes when the trains come to deport the ghetto residents to the concentration camps, and he later makes his way to America.

Throughout all the terror and death in the ghetto, the reader sees glimpses of love and beauty through the eyes of Misha. The title for the book comes from an incident when Misha and Janina find a milkweed plant growing in the middle of the ghetto. They enjoy watching the milkweed puffs flying skyward like angels:

> It was thrilling just to see a plant, a spot of green in the ghetto desert. The bird-shaped pods had burst and the puffs were spilling out, flying off. I cracked a pod from the stem and blew into the silk-lined hollow, sending the remaining puffs sailing, a snowy shower rising, vanishing into the clouds.[7]

Critics raved about *Milkweed*. The book won many awards, both in the United States and other countries, including the prestigious Golden Kite Award from the Society of Children's Book Writers and Illustrators. "Spinelli has written a powerfully moving story of survival," wrote Karin Snelson in a review for Amazon.com. "Readers will love Misha the dreamer and his wonderfully poetic observations of the world around him, his instinct to befriend a Jewish girl and her family, his impulse to steal food for a local orphanage and his friends in the ghetto, and his ability to delight in small things even surrounded by the horror of the Holocaust."[8]

Ginny Gustin, writing in *School Library Journal*, said, "This historical novel can be appreciated both by readers with previous knowledge of the Holocaust and by those who share Misha's innocence and will discover the horrors of this period in history along with him."[9]

After *My Daddy and Me* and *Milkweed* came a period with no new books. Spinelli still had more stories to write, but he found it harder and harder to carve out time at his writing desk. For one

Spinelli signs books at a promotional appearance.

thing, he wanted to spend time with Eileen, his six kids, and his sixteen grandkids. For another, many nonwriting demands competed for his attention. Top writers, like sports stars and performers, reach a point where so many people want them to do things that it becomes hard for them to focus on their primary activity.

For more than a decade, especially since the success of *Maniac Magee*, Spinelli has been a much sought-after speaker at schools, libraries, and educational conferences. He has been a featured speaker for the International Reading Association and the National Council of Teachers of English, where he sometimes speaks to more than a thousand educators at one time.

He also speaks at writers' conferences, where he uses his own experiences to encourage other writers to keep trying. Every other summer, he devotes a week to teaching at the Highlights Foundation Writers Workshop at Chautauqua, New York, where he makes presentations and serves as a mentor to aspiring writers.

Often in his speeches, he shares some of the humorous letters he receives from young readers. For instance, one youngster invited Spinelli to his school so he could meet their pet duck. A year later, the boy repeated the invitation with the comment that Spinelli should come soon because the duck was getting old.

In recent years, Spinelli also has become involved in the world of movies. The Nickelodeon Network released a film version of *Maniac Magee* in 2003, and the movie has aired on the Nickelodeon channel during Black History Month in February. *Milkweed*, *Wringer*, and *Stargirl* have also attracted the attention of film-makers. Adaptations for the stage are also in the works for a number of his books.

In 2005 Paramount Pictures flew Jerry and Eileen to Hollywood for meetings about the filming of *Stargirl*. "We love the screenplay and have high hopes it will become a fine film," Spinelli says.[10]

The Spinellis had a wonderful time in Hollywood, he adds, "but it was good to get home to those sixteen grandkids."[11]

Chapter 11

The Life of "A Person Who Writes"

So how does he do it? How has Jerry Spinelli kept turning out popular, award-winning books for so many years? Part of it is discipline. He tries to write every day, although with the distractions of kids and sixteen grandkids, speaking engagements, and other things such as movie deals, he sometimes finds it difficult to focus on writing. Not that he has any regrets. He likes to think of himself not as "a writer" but as "a person who writes."[1]

Jerry and Eileen both maintain writing offices

on the second floor of their home, which is in a small development in rural Chester County, Pennsylvania. A few years ago they downsized from the large home on two acres they had when their six kids lived at home.

Each day Jerry and Eileen walk upstairs to work. Jerry's office is spacious, with a desk, a computer, a filing cabinet, a supply closet, and bookshelves. The walls reflect his personality and life, with decorations ranging from a flower print by Georgia O'Keefe to two astronomy posters. He also has the original painting of the cover illustration of his first published novel, *Space Station Seventh Grade*, which Eileen found and presented to him as a birthday present one year. In addition, there's a color pencil portrait of Muhammad Ali, done by Ben Spinelli, their youngest son. Several of Jerry's awards, including the Newbery Medal for *Maniac Magee* and the Newbery Honor for *Wringer*, are also in the office.[2]

Spinelli likes to be comfortable when he writes. His favorite writing attire is "comfortable jeans, moccasins, and a flannel shirt," he said.[3]

Spinelli writes every morning from 10:00 A.M. to noon "barring family emergencies or other commitments such as attending conferences," he said.[4] He handles e-mail and phone messages before and after his writing time and in the evening.

Jerry also writes at night sometimes. That time is optional, however. What is not optional, though, is making sure that writing is a daily—or at least near daily—routine. "It is easy to put writing down and hard to pick it up," he noted.[5]

While Jerry and Eileen do not collaborate in a formal sense, they do support each other. Jerry shows his manuscripts to her chapter by chapter and takes seriously suggestions she may make. He returns the favor, providing feedback on her work as well. They are always honest with one another, even if they don't like something the other has written, but their reactions differ if they disagree with a critical comment. "I tend to ball up the paper and throw it away," Eileen said. "I tend to get more argumentative and defend my writing," Jerry said. But most of the time they agree, and all of the time they appreciate the support that comes from a spouse who understands just how difficult the writing process can be.[6]

"If there's something she doesn't like, I usually change it," Jerry said. "When I come to a snag, I often talk it over with her. More often than not, she untangles it for me."[7]

To get started each day, Spinelli reads a few pages from a book he finds meaningful. Then he sits down to write. He does not work from an outline. "I think it would suit my temperament because I'm a fastidious planner," he said. "I wish I could figure it out, plan it, and then just whip it off. But I can't. I can't seem to see around the corner until I get to the end of the block."[8]

Spinelli likens the act of moving through a book to playing a basketball game. The goal is to make a basket. "I know where I'm going," he said, "but

I don't know exactly how I'll get there from moment to moment." It all depends on how the defense is set up, where the other players are, and how the game is flowing.[9]

At this stage of his career, Spinelli can choose his projects carefully. He does not need to be as prolific as he did when he was first trying to scratch out a living from his writing. He can take his own advice to aspiring writers: "Write what you care about."[10]

That's what he did years ago, back in 1995—he wrote a book he cared about. He called it *Eggs*. But because an editor found a lot of fault with the manuscript, he lost faith in it and put it aside. As the years went by, he gradually forgot about it. Then one day Eileen said to him, "Hey, that book you wrote called *Eggs*. Do you still have it?"

"I think so," Jerry replied.

"Well, let me have a look at it," she said.

Spinelli found the forgotten manuscript at the bottom of a pile in his supply closet. He gave it to Eileen. She read it. She loved it. And so did his editor at Little, Brown. After more than a decade, *Eggs*—"my buried treasure," Spinelli calls it—will become a book.[11]

Spinelli is currently working on a sequel to *Stargirl*. He normally shies away from sequels because he often finds them disappointing. But Eileen suggested this book, and Jerry liked the idea of revisiting the character. Tentatively titled *Love, Stargirl*, the book picks up Stargirl's life a year later. The book takes the form of an extended letter or journal written through the course of a year. Stargirl addresses the writing to her former boyfriend, Leo.[12]

Spinelli still enjoys writing and still feels he has stories to tell. But he also makes time for his other favorite pursuits, which he lists as follows: Hang out with the grandkids. Play tennis. Pick berries. Swoon at the Milky Way. Read. Listen to country music. Ride trains.[13]

Spinelli also still enjoys contact with readers, and it remains a highlight of his writing life even after all these years. That contact may come through presentations at teacher conferences or at book signings, where he actually meets his fans one on one, if only for a moment or two.

One such occasion came at the IRA Annual Convention in Chicago, Illinois, in May 2006, where more than 20,000 educators gathered to learn more about the teaching of reading. Spinelli did autographing sessions over several days in the exhibit hall, then spoke to a packed banquet hall at a special author luncheon.

The audience listened intently as he told stories from his childhood and then showed how these stories later found their way into his books. He delighted the teachers by sharing letters—both funny and touching—that students had written to him. Several came from a girl named Heidi Jo, who wrote to him over a period of several years. Then she stopped writing, possibly having moved on to reading other, more adult novels. "I had been dumped," he said with a grin. "It's the way it is in

Spinelli speaks during an International Reading Association (IRA) convention in May 2006.

our business. They come and go—generations of kids."

Before and after his talk, Spinelli was surrounded by teachers who wanted to shake his hand, to have their pictures taken with him, or to have him sign a book for them. It meant a lot to them to meet in person an author who has meant so much to them and to their students.

Sitting at one of the front tables, Tricia Kraemer, a middle school teacher from Chicago, Illinois, said she has been a fan of Spinelli's for many years. Her students love his books—especially *Maniac Magee* and *Loser*. Seeing Spinelli was "one of the highlights of the whole conference," Kraemer said. "His books appeal to children. He has a range of characters. He also has a certain moral to the story. You walk away learning a little bit."[14]

Jessica Rogers, a fifth-grade teacher from Chicago, Illinois, went up to get her photo taken with Spinelli and came back with a huge smile on her face. She said her students especially like *Crash* and *Loser*. "His books inspire the kids to read and to write," she said. "His characters are so believable."[15]

Sometimes the contact with readers comes through letters. "It's rewarding when a teacher writes and says she was reading to her kids and the lunch bell rang, and they wanted her to keep reading," Spinelli said. One time he got a note from a mother whose daughter was in the hospital.

A book of his made the girl smile for the first time in weeks.[16]

On occasion he has done live Internet chats with students. There he sometimes shares his thoughts on writing. For instance, asked one time what supplies he would include in a writing kit, he replied: "A head full of memories. Notes of encouragement. Rejection slips (to use as confetti when I finally got published). Ideas. Good books."[17]

In addition to the Newbery Medal and Newbery Honor mentioned earlier, Spinelli's books have earned other awards and citations. He also has received some general honors, including being named an Honorary Doctor of Literature by McDaniel College and his alma mater, Gettysburg College.

He even got to visit the White House when he and Eileen were invited to participate in the National Book Festival in 2003. On the night before the festival, they were guests at a gala dinner held at a most appropriate location: the Library of Congress. There they were attended to by white-gloved Marines as they dined with fellow authors, members of the Cabinet, and President George W. Bush and First Lady Laura Bush.

Spinelli also takes pride in the fact that the South African government bought 600 copies of *Maniac Magee* to ease the transition from apartheid. And the U.S. State Department made arrangements to translate, print, and distribute *Stargirl* throughout the Middle East to help promote understanding between the West and that region of the world. "It's special," he concluded, "just to know that you're making a little bit of a difference."[18]

Spinelli has been making much more than a little bit of a difference for over twenty-five years, and it seems certain that his books will continue to entertain and inspire readers for many more years to come. Not bad for a writer who spent more than a decade trying to convince someone, anyone, that his work was worth publishing at all.

Jerry Spinelli's life proves the value of patience and persistence. It proves the value of preserving memories. For he possesses an amazing ability to take childhood memories and events and weave them together in ways that make them as fresh and meaningful today as they were when they first happened more than 50 years earlier.

Spinelli keeps those memories tucked away close by, ready for use at a moment's notice. He keeps creating new memories, too, through time spent with his family—especially his sixteen grandchildren. He makes sure not to let writing totally dominate his life. For, in the end, he and Eileen "are only writers 20 percent of the time," he said.[19]

Yet, in that 20 percent of his life, he has created unforgettable characters and books. What does he think are his greatest strengths as a writer? "I like to think I tell a good, interesting story that contains a message but is never overcome by it," he said. "I hope that in my dialogue the reader can hear his or her own voice coming off the page.

I try to give a sense of life in its variety, in which humor and disaster, sad and funny, up and down can all happen in the same day."[20]

Facts . . . memories . . . plot . . . details . . . dialogue—mix them all together and magical things happen, at least in the hands of a storyteller as masterful as Jerry Spinelli. For as he says in *Maniac Magee*, "the history of a kid is one part fact, two parts legend, and three parts snowball."[21]

In His Own Words

The following interview was conducted Saturday, August 6, 2005, at Jerry Spinelli's home near West Chester, Pennsylvania.

Question: Who is your favorite character?

Answer: Generally speaking, I've often thought my favorite characters tend to be the girls. I'm not sure why. I like Megin Tofer in *Who Put That Hair in My Toothbrush?* I've always been partial to her because she's such a feisty little kid. When she challenges her bigger brother at ice hockey with the line "Anytime, chump" is the favorite sentence of mine I've ever written.

Q: You tend to write about characters who are a bit out of the mainstream. Why is that?

A: I don't consciously write about "abnormal" characters. There's a very practical aspect to it. I would ask the readers, "If 100 people are running north in a herd and one is running south, which one are you going to want to read about and write about?" It's by the misfits among us that we measure ourselves. It's what illuminates us. Anyway, they're just more interesting.

Q: Several of your characters appear in more than one book. Is that a conscious choice on your part?

A: I like to thread a character or two or a theme or two or a place or two through many of my books. It's personally appealing to me. It gives me a sense that my work is a whole. There's also something vaguely appealing in plucking out a minor character and making something more of him. For instance, Maniac Magee appeared briefly in *Dump Days*. I don't *think* I knew at that point he would appear again later in another book.

Q: What advice do you have for young aspiring writers on developing their own style?

A: For young aspiring writers it's like a batting stance in baseball. There is no one right way. As Plato said, it's about knowing yourself. Design yourself around your own strengths.

Q: Talk a little bit about the importance of persistence to a writer.

A: Over a period of fifteen years, nobody wanted my four novels. What you can do is keep plugging away. I didn't quit. When I finished one book nobody wanted, I just started another one.

Q: Where do you get your ideas for your books?

A: The genesis varies from book to book. *Space Station Seventh Grade* began with a missing bag of fried chicken bones. I decided to write about it. For *Who Put That Hair in My Toothbrush?*, I zeroed in on two of our own kids, Molly and Jeffrey, who were always fighting.

There's a Girl in My Hammerlock was triggered by reading a story in the *Philadelphia Inquirer* about a girl wrestler. I took that as a springboard to make up my own story. *Milkweed* covered a lifelong interest. My advice to other writers is to write what you *care* about. I took my own advice.

Wringer came from reading year after year about a town's pigeon shooting event in the newspaper at the same time each year. It seemed like a natural situation for a book. The whole idea of raising money for the town through this intrigued me. I didn't see a way into the story for a long time, though, until one year I read about the wringers. Their job was to wring the necks of pigeons that were injured but not killed by the gunfire. A wringer boy—that was the key.

Q: How do you go about researching a book, and which book of yours required the most research?

A: I did more research for *Milkweed* than any other book. But I had been unknowingly doing research about that time period and Holocaust survivor stories for years. I also bought a wheelbarrow full of books from the Chester County Book Company. I spent three or four months doing research and reading. With every book, I reach a point where it becomes virtually impossible to keep thinking and ruminating and taking notes. Then it's time to write.

It's like high jumpers picturing themselves going up to the bar and clearing it. But sooner or later, they have to actually head for the bar and jump over it. I, too, reach the point where I have to do that.

Q: Describe your writing process.

A: To me, writing a book is not necessarily so much an academic or intellectual exercise as a physical one. I don't think of writing so much as a fine art as a performing art. I see it as moving through a story. I know where I want to go, but not always how to get there.

Q: You're a master with dialogue. What do you like about writing dialogue?

A: I love the look of a two-page spread where there's a lot of dialogue and a lot of white space. I love the fast, snappy pace of the story. People talking to each other; that's life!

Q: How long does it take you to write a book?

A: Typically, it takes the better part of a year to write a book. I don't write what I consider to be a draft. Sometimes I feel guilty. But I do work on a book for as long as it takes to get it right. For instance, I wrote eighty pages of *Maniac Magee* and didn't like it. I started again and wrote another eighty pages and didn't like it. Then I took a vacation from the project, and one evening the opening line just came to me: "They say Maniac Magee was born in a dump." That's a case when the muse came to me. Then I went ahead and wrote the book.

Q: What makes a good ending for a book?

A: Essentially, what you want is something that touches the reader—something with impact. Ideally, it should be the most moving part. That's what you leave the reader with. It's like a great ending to a movie.

Q: How do you celebrate when you finish a book?

A: When I finish a book, I spike my ball point pen and do an end zone dance like a football player.

Q: What kind of legacy do you hope to leave with your books?

A: Just knowing that my work will be around for years would satisfy me. One of the reasons I wanted to be a writer was the idea that this was something whereby I could leave a footprint behind. And when I think legacy, I think Stargirl Societies.

Q: How would you like to be remembered?

A: I write to touch the reader. I want to be remembered as an author who put my readers in touch with themselves, to recognize the humanity in themselves and others. A lot of what I write is about getting along. It's what's behind *Maniac Magee* and *Stargirl*. It's why Stargirl makes up her own Pledge of Allegiance.

Chronology

1936—*May 16*: Louis Anthony Spinelli and Lorna Mae Bigler are married in Norristown, Pennsylvania.

1941—*February 1:* Jerry Spinelli is born in Norristown, Pennsylvania.

1945—*July 29*: Bill Spinelli is born in Norristown, Pennsylvania.

1948—The Spinelli family moves to 802 George Street in the West End of Norristown, where they live for the next ten years.

1953—*April:* As a sixth grader, Jerry represents Hartranft Elementary School in the Montgomery County spelling bee. He lasts until the fourth round.

1953—*May:* Jerry wins the 50-yard dash championship for all Norristown grade schools.

1955—Jerry's Knee-Hi baseball team, Norristown Brick Company, wins the Pennsylvania state championship.

1956—January: Jerry is elected ninth-grade class president of Stewart Junior High School in Norristown, Pennsylvania.

1956—*May 25:* Jerry and his girlfriend, Judy Pierson, reign as king and queen of the ninth-grade prom.

1956—*June 19:* Jerry delivers the valedictory speech at Stewart Junior High School in Norristown, Pennsylvania.

1957—*October 11:* Norristown High School defeats

Lower Merion in a thrilling football game that leads to Jerry's first published work, a poem entitled "Goal to Go," which is published in the Norristown *Times Herald*.

1959—*June:* Jerry graduates from Norristown High School and goes off to Gettysburg College in Gettysburg, Pennsylvania, planning to become a writer. While there, he takes writing courses from a best-selling author named Kathrine Kressmann Taylor.

1963—Spinelli graduates from Gettysburg College with a degree in English.

1964—Spinelli earns a master's degree in The Writing Seminars program at the Johns Hopkins University in Maryland.

1965—Spinelli joins the Naval Air Reserve.

1966—Spinelli gets his first job with Chilton Company as a menswear and sporting goods editor for a magazine that goes to department stores. Soon he switches to another magazine that goes to design engineers. He stays in that job for twenty-three years.

1966—Spinelli meets Eileen Mesi, an aspiring writer who also works at Chilton Company.

1966—Spinelli conceives of the book idea that, thirty-four years later, will evolve into *Stargirl*.

1966—1980—Working at night and on his lunch hours, Spinelli writes four novels, none of which gets published.

1977—*May 21:* Marries Eileen Mesi.

1980—Spinelli's discovery of a bag of leftover chicken that had been reduced to bones leads to the development of his first published book.

1982—Spinelli's first book, *Space Station Seventh Grade*, is published by Little, Brown.

1984—*Who Put That Hair in My Toothbrush?* is published by Little, Brown.

1985—*Night of the Whale* appears, published by Little, Brown.

1986—*Jason and Marceline*, the sequel to *Space Station Seventh Grade*, is published by Little, Brown.

1988—*Dump Days* is published by Little, Brown. The book includes a fleeting mention of *Maniac Magee*.

1989—Spinelli quits his job at Chilton Company to become a full-time writer.

1990—*Maniac Magee* appears, published by Little, Brown. The book wins the Boston Globe/Horn Book Award. *The Bathwater Gang* is also published by Little, Brown.

1991—*Maniac Magee* wins the Newbery Medal, the highest honor in American children's literature. That same year, two more of his books also are published—*Fourth Grade Rats* (Scholastic) and *There's a Girl in My Hammerlock* (Simon & Schuster). Both of these books earn state reader awards.

1992—This year marks the publication of four more books: *The Bathwater Gang Gets Down to Business* (Little, Brown) and *Report to the Principal's Office*, *Who Ran My Underwear Up the Flagpole?*, and *Do the Funky Pickle* (Scholastic).

1993—*Picklemania!* is published by Scholastic.

1995—Random House publishes *Tooter Pepperday*.

1996—Knopf publishes *Crash*, about a bully who learns to change his ways. This book won honors from both educators and young readers.

1997—This year marks the publication of *The Library Card* (Scholastic) and *Wringer* (HarperCollins).

1998—*Wringer* is named a Newbery Honor Book. Knopf publishes Spinelli's book about his growing-up years, *Knots in My Yo-yo String: The Autobiography of a Kid*, and Random House publishes *Blue Ribbon Blues*, the sequel to *Tooter Pepperday*.

2000—Knopf publishes *Stargirl*, a book Spinelli first had the idea for thirty-four years earlier. *Stargirl* wins numerous awards. Also that year, Spinelli receives an honorary doctorate degree from McDaniel College in Maryland.

2002—HarperCollins publishes *Loser*, which wins numerous awards.

2003—Knopf publishes *My Daddy and Me*, Spinelli's first picture book. Also that year, Knopf publishes *Milkweed*, a grim story about a young orphan during the Holocaust. That year also marks the release of a Nickelodeon Network movie based on *Maniac Magee*.

2004—*Milkweed* wins the prestigious Golden Kite Award from the Society of Children's Book Writers and Illustrators. The book wins numerous other awards as well.

2005—Spinelli receives an honorary Doctor of Literature degree from Gettysburg College in Pennsylvania and the ALAN Award from the National Council of Teachers of English. Barnes and Noble comes out with a *Stargirl* gift card.

Chapter Notes

Chapter 1. A Writing Career Begins

1. Jerry Spinelli, *Knots in My Yo-yo String: The Autobiography of a Kid* (New York: Knopf, 1998), p. 142.
2. Ibid., pp. 143–144.
3. Ibid., p. 146.
4. Personal interview with Jerry Spinelli, August 6, 2005.
5. Ibid.

Chapter 2. Making Memories

1. Personal interview with Jerry Spinelli, August 6, 2005.
2. Jerry Spinelli, *Knots in My Yo-yo String: The Autobiography of a Kid* (New York: Knopf, 1998), pp. 2–3.
3. Ibid., pp. 69–70.
4. Ibid., p. 64.
5. Jerry Spinelli's website, n.d., <http://www.jerryspinelli.com/newbery_004.htm> (December 9, 2005).
6. "Jerry Spinelli," *Random House*, n.d., <http://www.randomhouse.com/features/jerryspinelli/> (November 18, 2005).
7. Spinelli, *Knots*, p. 90.
8. Don Gallo, "Jerry Spinelli," *Authors4Teens*, n.d., <http://www.Authors4Teens.com> (December 3, 2005).
9. Spinelli, *Knots*, p. 40.
10. Ibid., p. 93.

11. Interview on Eduplace website, n.d., <http://www.eduplace.com/kids/hmr/mtai/spinelli.html> (December 9, 2005).
12. Interview on *Kids Reads.com*, n.d., <http://www.kidsreads.com/authors/au-Spinelli-jerry.asp> (November 18, 2005).
13. Spinelli, *Knots*, p. 3.
14. Ibid., p. 32.
15. Ibid., p. 27.

Chapter 3: If at First You Don't Succeed

1. "In His Own Words: A Conversation with Jerry Spinelli," *Stargirl* (New York: Knopf, 2002), p. 7 of the "Readers' Guide."
2. "Authors & Books: Jerry Spinelli's Interview Transcript," *Scholastic*, n.d., <http://www2.schoolastic.com/teachers/authorsandbooks/events/spinelli/> (November 26, 2005).
3. Personal interview with Jerry Spinelli, August 6, 2005.
4. Diana L. Winarski, "Writing: Spinelli-Style," *Teaching Pre K-8*, October 1996, p. 42.
5. "Random House Children's Books Presents...Jerry Spinelli" brochure (New York: Random House, n.d.).
6. Personal interview with Jerry Spinelli, August 6, 2005.
7. "Authors & Books: Jerry Spinelli's Interview Transcript."
8. Don Gallo. "Jerry Spinelli interview," *Authors4Teens*, n.d., <http://www.Authors4Teens.com> (December 3, 2005).
9. Jane C. McFann. "Better Halves," *Reading Today*, August/September 2005, p. 23.
10. Ibid.

11. Winarski, p. 42.
12. Ibid.
13. Personal interview with Jerry Spinelli, August 6, 2005.
14. Ibid.
15. Jerry Spinelli, New York: Speech at the Society of Children's Book Writers midwinter meeting, February 4, 2005.
16. Ibid.
17. Ibid.

Chapter 4. Chicken Bones Bring Success at Last

1. Jerry Spinelli, *Space Station Seventh Grade* (Boston: Little, Brown and Company, 1982), p. 1.
2. Personal interview with Jerry Spinelli, August 6, 2005.
3. Ibid.
4. Ibid.
5. John Keller, "Jerry Spinelli," *The Horn Book Magazine*, July/August 1991, p. 435.
6. Don Gallo. "Jerry Spinelli Interview," *Authors4Teens*, n.d., <http://www.Authors4Teens.com> (December 3, 2005).
7. Ibid.
8. Marilyn H. Karrenbrock, Review of *Space Station Seventh Grade* in *ALAN Review*, Greenwood Publishing Company, <http://pub.greenwood.com> (December 3, 2005).
9. Personal correspondence from Jerry Spinelli, April 28, 2005.
10. "Jerry Spinelli's Interview Transcript," Scholastic, n.d., <http://books.scholastic.com/teachers/authorsandbooks/authorstudies/authorhome.jsp?authorID=90&&displayName=Interview%20Transcript> (December 3, 2005).

Chapter 5. More Books and a Daring Decision

1. Personal interview with Jerry Spinelli, August 6, 2005.
2. "Jerry Spinelli," *Kids Reads.com*, n.d., <http://www.kidsreads.com/authors/au-Spinelli-jerry.asp.> (December 12, 2005).
3. "Jerry Spinelli's Interview Transcript," *Scholastic*, n.d., <http://teacher.scholastic.com/authorsandbooks/events/spinelli/transcript.htm> (December 12, 2005).
4. Personal interview with Jerry Spinelli, August 6, 2005.
5. Judy Rowen, review of *Who Put That Hair in My Toothbrush?*, *Children's Literature*, n.d., <http://www.childrenslit.com/f_jerryspinelli.html> (December 12, 2005).
6. Barbara J. Craig, Review of *Who Put That Hair in My Toothbrush?* in *ALAN Reviews*, *Authors4Teens*, n.d., <http://www.Authors4Teens.com> (December 12, 2005).
7. Gloria Miklowitz, "Young Adult Books: Teen-Age Love from a Male Viewpoint," *Los Angeles Times*, May 9, 1987, part 5, p. 6.
8. Review of *Dump Days* from *Publishers Weekly*. *Amazon.com*, n.d., <http://www.amazon.com> (December 12, 2005).
9. Jerry Spinelli, *Dump Days* (Boston: Little, Brown and Company, 1988), p. 36.
10. Personal interview with Jerry Spinelli, August 6, 2005.
11. Ibid.
12. Susan Hepler, Review of *The Bathwater Gang* in *School Library Journal*. *Amazon.com*, n.d., <http://www.amazon.com> (December 12, 2005).

Chapter 6. A Marvelous Maniac

1. Jerry Spinelli, "Catching Maniac Magee," *The Reading Teacher*, Vol. 45, No. 3, p. 174.
2. Ibid.
3. Ibid.
4. Ibid., p. 175.
5. Personal interview with Jerry Spinelli, August 6, 2005.
6. *The Reading Teacher*, p. 176.
7. Jerry Spinelli, *Maniac Magee* (Boston: Little, Brown and Company, 1990), p. 1.
8. Personal interview with Jerry Spinelli, August 6, 2005.
9. *The Reading Teacher*, p. 176.
10. Personal interview with Jerry Spinelli, August 6, 2005.
11. Review of *Maniac Magee* appearing in *Publishers Weekly*, *Amazon.com*, n.d., <www.amazon.com> (December 14, 2005).
12. Louise Sherman, Review of *Maniac Magee* appearing in *School Library Journal*, *Amazon.com*, n.d., <www.amazon.com> (December 14, 2005).
13. Review of *Maniac Magee* appearing in *The New York Times Book Review*, *Amazon.com*, n.d., <www.amazon.com> (December 14, 2005).
14. Mona Kirby, "Jerry Spinelli." *Author's Corner*, n.d., <http://www.carr.org/authco/spinelli-j.htm> (December 14, 2005).
15. Personal interview with Jerry Spinelli, August 6, 2005.
16. Ibid.
17. Ibid.
18. Ibid.

Chapter 7. Not Resting on His Laurels

1. Jerry Spinelli, *Fourth Grade Rats* (New York: Scholastic, Inc., 1991), p. 1.

2. Personal interview with Jerry Spinelli, August 6, 2005.

3. Review of *Fourth Grade Rats* from *Publishers Weekly*, *Amazon.com*, n.d., <http://www. amazon.com> (December 15, 2005).

4. Pamela T. Bomboy, review of *Report to the Principal's Office* from *School Library Journal*. *Amazon.com*, n.d., http://www.amazon.com. (December 15, 2005).

5. Personal interview with Jerry Spinelli, August 6, 2005.

6. Ted Hipple, review of *There's a Girl in My Hammerlock* in *ALAN Reviews*. *Greenwood Publishing*, n.d., <http://pub.greenwood. com/servlet/A4TAlan?action=titles&title=1192> (December 15, 2005).

7. Personal interview with Jerry Spinelli, August 6, 2005.

8. Review of *Tooter Pepperday* in *Booklist*. *Amazon.com*, n.d., <http://www.amazon.com> (December 15, 2005).

9. Review of *Crash* in *Publishers Weekly*. *Amazon.com*, n.d., <http://www.amazon.com> (December 15, 2005).

10. Connie Tyrrell Burns, Review of *Crash* in *School Library Journal*, *Amazon.com*, n.d., <http:// www.amazon.com> (December 15, 2005).

11. Don Gallo, "Jerry Spinelli interview," *Authors4Teens*, n.d., <http://www.Authors4Teens. com> (December 15, 2005).

12. "Children's Choices," *International Reading Association*, n.d., <http://www.reading.org/resources/tools/choices_childrens.html> (December 15, 2005).

13. Debra Dorfman and Lorraine Occhini, Scholastic interview with Jerry Spinelli on *The Library Card* (New York: Scholastic, 1997, tape recording).

14. Mary Sue Preissner, Review of *The Library Card*, *Children's Literature.com*, n.d., <http://www.childrenslit.com/f_jerryspinelli.html> (December 15, 2005).

15. Review of *The Library Card* in *Kirkus Reviews*. *Amazon.com*, n.d., <http://www.amazon.com> (December 15, 2005).

16. Personal interview with Jerry Spinelli, August 6, 2005.

17. Marilyn Courtot, Review of *Wringer*, *Children's Literature*, n.d., <http://www.childrenslit.com/f_jerryspinelli.html> (December 15, 2005).

18. Review of *Wringer*, *Amazon.com*, n.d., <http://www.amazon.com> (December 15, 2005).

Chapter 8. Talking About the Memories

1. Don Gallo, "Jerry Spinelli Interview," *Authors4Teens*, n.d., <http://www.Authors4Teens.com> (December 17, 2005).

2. Jerry Spinelli, *Knots in My Yo-yo String* (New York: Knopf, 1998). p. 148.

3. "An Interview with Jerry Spinelli," *Reading Is Fundamental,* n.d., <http://www.rif.org/readingplanet/content/spinelli.mspx> (December 17, 2005).

4. Review from *Publishers Weekly* of *Knots in My Yo-yo String*, *Amazon.com*, n.d., <http://www.amazon.com> (December 17, 2005).

Chapter 9. A Stargirl and a Boy Called Loser

1. Personal interview with Jerry Spinelli, August 6, 2005.
2. Jerry Spinelli, "In His Own Words: A Conversation With Jerry Spinelli" in *Stargirl* (New York: Knopf, 2000), p. 8 of special section.
3. Personal interview with Jerry Spinelli, August 6, 2005.
4. Ibid.
5. Reviews excerpted in the back matter of *Stargirl* (New York: Knopf, 2000).
6. Jerry Spinelli, "In His Own Words: A Conversation With Jerry Spinelli," p. 6 of special section.
7. Ibid.
8. Jerry Spinelli, *Loser* (New York: HarperCollins, 2002), p. 106.
9. Don Gallo. "Jerry Spinelli Interview," *Authors4Teens*, n.d., <http://www.Authors4Teens.com> (December 17, 2005).
10. "Scholastic's Online Reading Club: Let's Talk About *Loser*," *Scholastic*, n.d., <http://teacher.scholastic.com/authorsandbooks/events/spinelli/transcript.htm> (December 17, 2005).
11. Review of *Loser* from *Publishers Weekly*, *Amazon.com*, n.d., <http://www.amazon.com> (December 17, 2005).

Chapter 10. Milkweed, Movies, and More

1. Personal interview with Jerry Spinelli, August 6, 2005.
2. Karin Snelson, Review of *My Daddy and Me*, Amazon.com, n.d., <http://www.amazon.com> (December 22, 2005).

3. Leslie Barban, Review of *My Daddy and Me* for *School Library Journal*, *Amazon.com*, n.d., <http://www.amazon.com> (December 22, 2005).
4. Jane C. McFann, "Better Halves," *Reading Today*, August/September 2005, p. 23.
5. Personal interview with Jerry Spinelli, August 6, 2005.
6. Ibid.
7. Jerry Spinelli, *Milkweed* (New York: Knopf, 2003), p. 143.
8. Karin Snelson, Review of *Milkweed*, *Amazon.com*, n.d., <http://www.amazon.com> (December 22, 2005).
9. Ginny Gustin, review of *Milkweed* for *School Library Journal*, *Amazon.com*, n.d., <http://www.amazon.com> (December 22, 2005).
10. Personal correspondence with Jerry Spinelli, January 9, 2006.
11. Ibid.

Chapter 11. The Life of "A Person Who Writes"

1. Personal correspondence, January 9, 2006.
2. Don Gallo, "Jerry Spinelli Interview," *Authors4Teens*, n.d., <http://www.Authors4Teens.com> (December 16, 2005).
3. Mona Kirby, "Jerry Spinelli," *Author's Corner*, n.d., <http://www.carr.org/authco/spinelli-j.htm> (December 14, 2005).
4. Jane C. McFann, "Better Halves," *Reading Today*, August/September 2005, p. 23.
5. Ibid.
6. Ibid.
7. Gallo.

8. Personal interview with Jerry Spinelli, August 6, 2005.

9. Ibid.

10. Ibid.

11. Personal correspondence with Jerry Spinelli, January 9, 2006.

12. Personal interview with Jerry Spinelli, August 6, 2005.

13. Jerry Spinelli's website, <http://www.jerryspinelli.com/newbery_004.htm> (December 16, 2005).

14. Personal interview with Tricia Kraemer, May 4, 2006.

15. Personal interview with Jessica Rogers, May 4, 2006.

16. Personal interview with Jerry Spinelli, August 6, 2005.

17. Transcript of "Authors Live with Jerry Spinelli," *Teachervision*, February 26, 2002, <http://www.teachervision.fen.com> (December 16, 2005).

18. Personal interview, August 6, 2005.

19. McFann, p. 23.

20. Gallo.

21. Jerry Spinelli, *Maniac Magee* (New York: Little, Brown, and Company, 1990), p. 2.

Glossary

accolades—Praise.

adaptation—The taking of something from one form and adapting it to another, such as making a book into a movie or play.

agent—A person who represents an author's works to publishers.

allegorical—Like an allegory; a story that has a message.

aspiring—Striving or working toward something.

collaborate—To work together to do something.

confiscated—Taken.

dialogue—Conversation, especially in a book, play, movie, or television program.

fastidiously—Carefully.

gumption—Courage, nerve.

Holocaust—The killing of millions of European Jews and others by the Nazis during World War II.

imperative—Very important, crucial.

maniac—Someone who is insane or who acts in a wild manner; someone who is very enthusiastic about something.

narration—The telling of a story.

Newbery Medal—An award given each year for the most outstanding children's book published in the United States.

premise—A statement or principle that is accepted as true or taken for granted; the basis upon which something is built.

prolific—Very productive or producing a large quantity.

protagonist—The hero in a story.

recollections—Rememberings.

rejection—When something, such as a book manuscript, is turned down.

revisions—Changes, such as are made to a manuscript to make it better.

stereotypical—Creating an overly simple picture of a person, group, or thing.

thesis—The formal project work that a person submits to qualify for a master's degree.

unconventional—Not fitting normal conventions or ways of doing things, different.

unpretentious—Not putting on airs; acting in a very natural manner.

unsolicited—Something that has not been asked for, such as when an author sends a manuscript to a publisher without being invited to do so.

valedictory—Relating to the valedictorian, or number one student in a class.

Major Works

1990—*Maniac Magee*
1996—*Crash*
1997—*Wringer*
1998—*Knots in My Yo-yo String: The Autobiography*
  of a Kid
2000—*Stargirl*
2002—*Loser*
2003—*Milkweed*

Selected Additional Works
1982—*Space Station Seventh Grade*
1984—*Who Put That Hair in My Toothbrush?*
1985—*Night of the Whale*
1986—*Jason and Marceline*
1988—*Dump Days*
1990—*The Bathwater Gang*
1991—*There's a Girl in My Hammerlock*
  Report to the Principal's Office
1992—*The Bathwater Gang Gets Down to Business*
  Who Ran My Underwear Up the Flagpole?
  Do the Funky Pickle
1993—*Picklemania*
1995—*Tooter Pepperday*
1997—*The Library Card*
1998—*Blue Ribbon Blues*
2003—*My Daddy and Me*

Further Reading

Books

Seidman, David. *Jerry Spinelli*. New York: Rosen Central, 2004.

Spinelli, Jerry. *Knots in My Yo-yo String: The Autobiography of a Kid*. New York: Knopf, 1998.

Weiss, Jaqueline Shacter. *Profiles in Children's Literature: Discussions with Authors, Artists, and Editors*. Lenham, Md.: Scarecrow Press, 2001.

Video

Good Conversation!: A Talk with Jerry Spinelli. Tim Podell Productions. Bohemia, N.Y.: Rainbow Educational Video, 1994.

Internet Addresses

Jerry Spinelli's website
http://www.jerryspinelli.com

Random House's Jerry Spinelli page
http://www.randomhouse.com/features/jerryspinelli/

Scholastic's online interview with Jerry Spinelli
http://www.books.scholastic.com/teachers

Index